FROGGY'S BIRTHDAY WISH

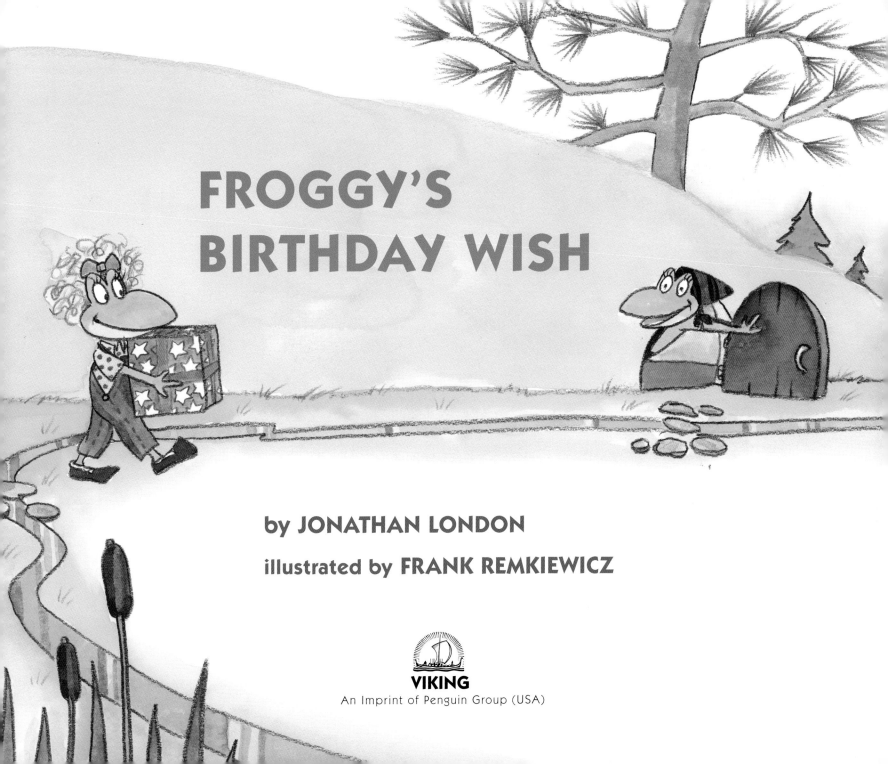

FROGGY'S BIRTHDAY WISH

by **JONATHAN LONDON**

illustrated by **FRANK REMKIEWICZ**

VIKING
An Imprint of Penguin Group (USA)

For Sean, Steph, Aaron, Christie, Jessica, Alegra, Eli, and sweet Maureen
—J.L.

For Jim for making Froggy look so good
—F.R.

VIKING
Published by the Penguin Group
Penguin Group (USA) Inc.
375 Hudson Street
New York, New York 10014, U.S.A.

USA * Canada * UK * Ireland * Australia
New Zealand * India * South Africa * China

penguin.com
A Penguin Random House Company

First published in the United States of America by Viking, an imprint of Penguin Young Readers Group, 2015

LIBRARY OF CONGRESS CATALOGING-IN-PUBLICATION DATA IS AVAILABLE
ISBN: 978-0-670-01572-6

Manufactured in China

10   9   8   7   6   5   4   3   2   1

It was the night before
Froggy's birthday,
and Froggy was excited.
"Look! The moon!" cried Froggy.
"It looks like an orange piñata!"
And Froggy made a birthday wish.

"FRROOGGYY!"

called his mom in the morning.
"Wha-a-a-t?"
"Time for breakfast, dear!"

Froggy bounced on his bed, and sang:
"Happy birthday to meeeeeeeee!
Happy birthday to meeeeeeeee!
Happy birthday, dear Frrooggyy.
Happy birthday to meeeeeeeeee!"

Then he got dressed—*zip! zoop! zup! zut! zut! zut! zat!*—

and flopped into the kitchen—*flop flop flop.*
"Are we having something . . . special?"
asked Froggy.
"Uhhh, no, dear. Why do you ask?"
"Oh, I don't know," said Froggy.

"Are you doing anything special today, Dad?"
"Um, not really. Why do you ask?"
Then Froggy turned to Polly. "Well,
what do you have to say, Polly?"
"Poo-poo on you!" *Hee hee!*

Froggy ate his bowl of cereal and flies,
and wondered,
What if my family FORGOT my birthday?

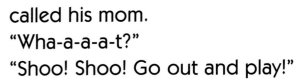

called his mom.
"Wha-a-a-t?"
"Shoo! Shoo! Go out and play!"

So Froggy flopped over to Max's—
flop flop flop . . .
and banged on the door.
"Max! Max!" he shouted.
But nobody was home.
"Oh no!" cried Froggy.
"What if Max forgot my birthday?"

Then he went over to Matthew's . . .
but nobody was home.
"Oh no!" cried Froggy.
"What if Matthew forgot my birthday?"

Then he went over to Travis's . . .
but nobody was home.
"Oh no!" cried Froggy.
"What if Travis forgot my birthday?"

So he dragged himself home—
zloooop!—wondering,
"What if EVERYBODY forgot my birthday?
So much for my birthday wish!
Sigh."

Everybody was there!
Max, Matthew, Travis.
Even Frogilina.

Frogilina said, "I bet you were worried that everybody forgot your birthday."

"Not me!" said Froggy.

Froggy still had hopes for his birthday wish, but first . . .

he and his friends
played pin-the-tail-on-the-donkey.
(Froggy almost pinned the tail
on Max's mother's bottom!)
"Oops!"
Arf! laughed Doggy.

Now it was time for the birthday cake.
And here came Mom with all the
candles burning,
and everybody sang:

"Happy birthday to you!
Happy birthday to you!
Happy birthday, dear Frrooogyy . . .
Happy birthday to yoooooouuu!"

This was the moment Froggy had been waiting for!
He made his wish . . .
took a BIG breath . . .
and blew out all the candles—*whooooooooosh!*
After they gobbled down the cake, Mom announced,
"Time to open presents!"

First, Froggy ripped open a present from Max.
(With a little help from Doggy.)
"A skateboard!" he shouted, and hopped on—
zoom! CRRRAAAAASH!
He knocked over the punch bowl.
"Oops!" said Froggy.

Then he ripped open a present from Matthew.
"A scooter!" he shouted, and hopped on—*zing!*
CRRRAAAAASH!
He nearly knocked over the fish bowl.

And then he ripped open a present from Travis.
"A pogo stick!" he shouted,
and hopped on—*boing! boing! boing!*—
and hit his head on the ceiling—*bonk!*—
and fell down.
But he still hadn't got his wish.

Finally Frogilina said, "I have a surprise
for you, Froggy. Close your eyes."
And what do you think she gave him?
A big, fat . . .

piñata! Like an orange moon!
"Yippee!" cried Froggy. And he sang,
"I got my wiiiiish! I got my wiiiiish!"

So Froggy flopped outside—*flop flop flop*—
and Dad hung the piñata from the tree
and tied a bandanna over his eyes.
Then Froggy swung the bat . . .

and missed—*zwish!*
He swung again—*zwish!*
And on his third swing . . .

WHACK!

the piñata flew up, up, up . . .
then dropped down,
down, down . . .

and burst open on
Froggy's head—*ZPLAT!*
"Oops!" cried Froggy,
looking more red in
the face than green.

"Candy! Candy!" yelled Frogilina.
"Candy for everyone!"

And everyone dived in.
Even Doggy.
"Well, I got my wish!" cried Froggy.

"And it was filled with chocolate-covered flies! YUM!"— *munch crunch munch.*

"Num num!" said Pollywogilina, stuffing her face with candy. "Happy BURPday, Fwoggy!"—*BURP!* And everybody laughed.

Even Doggy.